TEDD ARNOLD

HUGGLY
GOES TO SCHOOL

SCHOLASTIC INC.

Cartwheel
B·O·O·K·S ®

New York   Toronto   London   Auckland   Sydney
Mexico City   New Delhi   Hong Kong

To Lisa Kelly and all the great children, parents, teachers, and staff
at Parley Coburn Elementary School
— T. A.

ISBN: 0-439-13499-4

Copyright © 2000 by Tedd Arnold.
All rights reserved. Published by Scholastic Inc.
HUGGLY and THE MONSTER UNDER THE BED are trademarks and/or registered trademarks of Tedd Arnold.
SCHOLASTIC, CARTWHEEL BOOKS and associated logos are trademarks and/or registered trademarks of Scholastic Inc.

Library of Congress Cataloging-in-Publication Data available

12 11 10 9 8 7 6 5 4 3 2 1   00 01 02 03 04 05 06

Printed in the U.S.A.
First printing, September 2000

Huggly was about to climb up and play in the people child's bedroom when Booter and Grubble found him. "Hi, Huggly," said Booter. "Come play hide-and-seek with us."

"Okay," said Huggly. "Hey, Grubble, it's our turn to hide."

"Yeah," said Grubble. "And guess what, Booter. You *never* win hide-and-seek!"

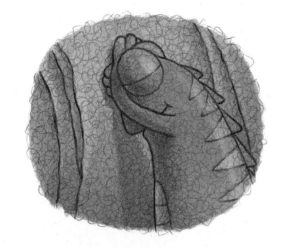

"Until now!" said Booter. "Ready?" She turned and covered her eyes. "One, two, three . . ."

Huggly and Grubble scrambled away, zigzagging through a maze of caverns. Suddenly, Huggly stopped at a dark hole. "This looks good."

"It's big enough for me, too," said Grubble.

They climbed in and discovered a tunnel and dusty wooden steps. There was a hatch in the ceiling. They knew that hatches always opened up under people beds.

"Let's take a look," said Huggly.

They climbed up and peeked out from under the bed. "What kind of place is this?" Huggly asked. They saw strange furniture and several doors.

"Maybe they have slime pits here," said Grubble. "Want to explore?"

"I do if you do," said Huggly.

Huggly opened a big jar of puffy white balls.

Grubble found a clanky contraption.

They both found boxes with sticky things.

Huggly opened one of the doors and cautiously stepped out into a long, empty tunnel. Suddenly, a bell rang overhead. Doors banged open somewhere, and they heard lots of people coming. *We set off an alarm! We're going to get caught!* thought Huggly. "Let's get back under the bed!" he cried.

Just then, a big people person came through another door
near the bed. "Oh, no! We can't go that way!" whispered Huggly.
They hurried along the tunnel looking for a hiding place.
At that moment, a huge crowd of people children
came around a corner.

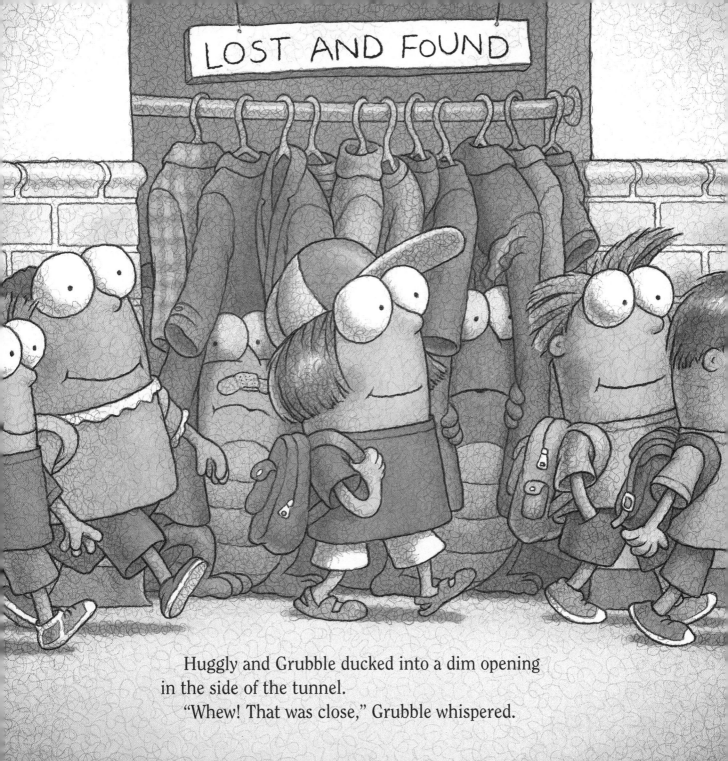

Huggly and Grubble ducked into a dim opening
in the side of the tunnel.
"Whew! That was close," Grubble whispered.

"Hey, look at all this stuff!" said Huggly. Hanging around them were the things that people children wear. "We could disguise ourselves until we can get back under that bed."

Huggly and Grubble weren't sure how to wear everything, but they did their best.

Gradually, the big tunnel grew quiet as the crowds of people children disappeared through different doorways.
"All clear," said Huggly. "Let's go!"
They tiptoed back toward the room with the bed.

But before they reached the door, a loud voice
boomed from behind them. "THERE YOU ARE!"
Huggly and Grubble froze in their tracks. *Yikes!*
thought Huggly. *Now we're caught for sure!*

"I'm Principal Parley," a big people person said. "I was expecting two new students tomorrow. But here you are today! Wasn't your mother bringing you?"

Huggly and Grubble were scared speechless.

"Oh, never mind! Let's go meet your teacher."

Principal Parley led Huggly and Grubble to a noisy room. "Have a nice day and do your best!" she said, and left them with a teacher person named Mrs. Coburn.

"Look, boys and girls," said Mrs. Coburn. "Our two new students are here. Just in time for math! Today, we'll practice counting to ten." Everyone counted on their fingers. Huggly and Grubble never made it to ten.

"Okay, class," Mrs. Coburn announced. "Gather around for story time." The story was exciting. But Huggly and Grubble were the only ones who cheered when the cave monster flattened a village.

Next, it was time for art. Mrs. Coburn passed out paper and asked everyone to draw pictures of their mothers.

All day long, Huggly and Grubble had so much fun they completely lost track of time.

Finally, on their way back from the library, Huggly said, "School is great, but maybe we should think about getting back home now."

"Good idea," said Grubble.

They slipped past the classroom door and hurried down the big tunnel.

"Aha! There you are again!" It was Principal Parley, right behind them. "I was correct! Your mother *was* supposed to bring you. And, finally, here she is! I brought her to see your classroom."

Huggly and Grubble were too afraid to move.
A people mother would know they were not real
children! *Oh, no!* thought Huggly. *Now we're
really caught for sure.*

They slowly turned around to face her.

"Hello, children," Booter said in a high voice. "The school day is nearly over. Why don't I just take you home now."

"Fine idea!" said Principal Parley, waving good-bye. "See you tomorrow, bright and early!"

Booter, Huggly, and Grubble hurried toward the room with the bed. But Principal Parley's voice stopped them again. "You must be confused. The school's front door is right down the hall."

"My mistake," Booter mumbled. Uncertainly, she led Huggly and Grubble outside.

They stood on the steps of the school and looked around.
"How do we get home without a bed?" asked Grubble.
"I have no idea," said Booter. "It took all my brainpower
just to find you two. Now we're in real trouble!"
Suddenly a bell rang, the doors behind them burst open,
and hundreds of children poured out of the school.

"I have an idea!" said Huggly, pointing into the crowd. "I recognize that people child! I've played in his bedroom before. Let's just follow him home and climb under his bed."

And they did.

Safely back in their own world again, Booter said,
"Guess what!"

"What?" asked Grubble and Huggly.

"I WON HIDE-AND-SEEK!" she announced as
she ran down the tunnel, laughing all the way.